DEATH'S
RETRIBUTION

DEATH'S RETRIBUTION

JOHN W. SMITH

DEATH'S RETRIBUTION

Book and Cover design by Nemo Designs

ISBN: 978-0-9891810-7-5

First Edition: July 2018

0 9 8 9 1 8 1 0 7 3

Acknowledgements

I want to thank all the people who helped make this short story possible. Writing it was easy, but it took an army of people to make this book worth reading.

The past several months has included seven members of a Critique Group going through each chapter of this work. Thank you to Susan Bryant, Doug Callies, Pat Flowers, Heather Hinson, Ticia Metheney, Jessi Meyer, and Jacki Meyer. In addition, thank you to the members of Ocular Voices writers group for listening to the story and offering suggestions to bolster the tension.

My Beta readers included Linda Bemis, Jaime Cancio, and Howard Smith.

To my Cover designer, formatter and Fellow Veteran Shannon Nemechek of Nemo Designs Thank you!

Last but not least a Big Thank You to Sandy Maue, founder of The Editeers, a small specialized group of independent editors. Sandy has the patience of a saint to work with me week after week.

And my biggest thank you is to all the readers to buy this book and enjoy it. Please post a review on Amazon.

CONTENTS

CHAPTER ONE

It was a cold February afternoon when the priest finish his prayer for the dead. People walked by the casket and bid their final farewells to the widow. They abandoned her, one by one, including the priest, who blessed her and departed. She stood at the edge of the grave, alone, head bowed. Her heavy cape and long black dress provided little protection from the biting wind, pressing her veil against her face. Her shoulders hunched in a silent sob.

From the corner of her eye, Sylvia Davlen realized there were no stragglers.

The mist turned to fog which found and soaked into her clothing. She withdrew the black hanky used to dab away her tears from her face and wadded it in her hand.

"Silk or not, it's rubbing my eye raw." She said to herself, as she glanced at her watch. "Another ten minutes and I am out of here. Any remaining on-lookers will be satisfied that I paid my proper respects."

She understood having to endure the sermon at the church and again at the gravesite, but this god awful weather was almost more than she could bear. She shivered as the dampness settled into her bones. She looked forward to the warmth of her home, soaking in a hot bath until she felt human again.

Sylvia knew, from past experience, that she just couldn't walk away. As a loving wife, the town's people expected a certain amount of grief demonstrated at the gravesite. Even in this weather, there were certain people in town who would watched her. They suspected she married for money and that she killed him. This performance would make the most suspicious of these petty people keep their gossip to themselves. Her biggest critics would stay quiet about their suspicions. The rest of the town would believe she was nothing more than a proper wife.

"At last," she sighed to herself, standing up straight and squaring her shoulders, "time to settle affairs like a good wife and get the hell out of this god-forsaken town."

An opaque figure formed along the tree line and moved toward the gravesite. A deep, baritone voice whispered through the fog. "Sylvia, why aren't you smiling and dancing for joy?"

A stranger walking within vapor. She studied the shape and size of the interloper in an attempt to identify the man behind the voice. "I just buried my husband, why would I be jumping for joy and smiling? Have you no heart or compassion?" She responded in anger.

As the form moved closer, Sylvia squinted yet she found no identifying features, no hair, beard or mustache.

She considered stepping across the grave to get a better look, but changed her mind. *I will sink to my knees in mud, ruin a good pair of shoes and be stuck here until a grounds keeper makes his rounds tomorrow.*

"I don't know who you are since you are hiding your identity, but if you are trying to scare me, I've seen far worse in my life and you are nothing more than an irritating distraction keeping me from my carriage."

His deep laughter reminded her of large rocks falling down a mountain side and held an ominous tone. "Come now, Sylvia, I have kept my eye on you since you killed your first animal … we both know the truth. You are not heart-broken. For the fifth time in twelve years you have buried a husband. I know you are already counting the money you intend to collect before you disappear."

She gasped, "I ... I don't know what you're talking about. Harold was a kind man, and he was good to me. He was my soul mate. How dare you say such a thing."

"Ah, Sylvia, I know you. I have followed your adventures for most of your life. You are a planner and always escape without a trace, but this time will be different. You are in for a few surprises."

When he reached the edge of the grave, she shivered as a chill raked her spine.

"You did not know Harold sold the foundry just before you began poisoning him. He was retiring due to declining health and wanted to spend his last days with you. You are far richer than you dreamed."

He floated from the head to the foot of the grave and back again, as though pacing. He appeared to enjoy torturing her. "You will receive all the details at the reading of the will."

Sylvia stepped to the foot of the grave. "I already know the details, I wrote it."

The figure glided to the headstone, keeping his distance, as he continued to frustrate and anger her. "Oh do you?"

She shrugged. "The money doesn't matter to me. My plans are to remain the lady of Davlen House. I will establish my own power and influence within the community. I will set a shining example of proper living and caring for the people as my dear Harold did for years." Raising her chin, she challenged the voice behind the fog.

The form leaned over the headstone, his face pushed closer to the edge of the mist. Mysterious water droplets fell from his cowl, blocking most of her view. She saw a few details. His eye sockets were as black as night, there was no hair to be seen on his head or eye brows. It was more frustrating than frightful.

"Come now, I know you planned to pull every bit of coin out of the accounts, sell the foundry for next to nothing and leave town. Harold's children will get nothing. You saw to that when you convinced him to disown them."

Sylvia focused on the mist. "How can you say such things? His children are grown and successful on their own. They have no need of his money or assets."

The mist seemed to shake as the voice laughed. "What about personal things, the grandfather clock and other mementos that bring fond memories to them?"

Sylvia huffed. "If they want any of that crap, they can come to the auction."

"Ah, Sylvia, my cold hearted bitch. I think this is why I love you," he said.

With the last comment, she turned on her heel, head

bowed, and marched toward the cemetery gate.

"We will speak again Sylvia." His voice said clearly in her head. "You will visit the grave every day until the last check is signed and given to you. We will talk of your past adventures, loves, and soul mates."

She ignored the voice as she scraped mud and grass off the bottom of her shoes when she reached the walkway. She turned and dropped her right hand to her side as she brandished her middle finger at the specter. Glancing over her shoulder, he was nowhere to be seen.

"Ah Sylvia, you are indeed a treasure. We will become best friends." His voice whispered in her head. "You will grow to love me for all the wrong reasons."

Sylvia passed through the main gate of the cemetery and entered the first available carriage. The rain ceased to fall as the late sun broke through the clouds.

CHAPTER TWO

Sylvia fumed as the carriage made its way to the mansion at the top of the hill. *The nerve of that ghost or specter or whatever, hinting about my past. He has no idea who he is dealing with. I am Sylvia Davlen, and I now own most of this town.* She thought about part of his conversation and wondered … *How does he know about my past marriages? How did I not know he has watched me since I was a child? At least he didn't call me by any of my other names. He seems content to focus on the current me. I'll get him to give up his secrets and ruin the bastard.*

The carriage pulled around the circle driveway, where the portico protected her from the wind as she climbed out unassisted. Her anger grew as she stomped up the stairs and crossed the porch in three strides. Herman, the man servant, opened the door as her foot touched the top step. She entered the foyer and nodded at him with a scowl on her face. Her head snapped toward the sitting room when she heard light laughter and voices floating into the entryway.

"No respect for the grieving widow," she whispered to herself. "I'll have their asses out of my home in an instant."

She once again applied her grief mask, slumped her shoulders, and shuffled toward the sitting room. She rubbed her eyes making them appear red and felt her cheeks for dried tear stains.

Sylvia stopped in her tracks, straightening her back. Her shoulders tensed as her sad face turned reddened with anger. Her eyes narrowed, on her two step-children, their spouses, and grungy, mutant rug rats. As they turned their attention to Sylvia, her jaws lock and her hands clinched into fists.

Simon, Harold's son stood and walked to her. Holding out his arms, he embraced her in a compassionate hug. "Sylvia, I am as sorry for your loss, as we are for ours. If there is anything any of us can do to help you through this time, just ask."

By then Annabelle, Harold's daughter, reached the couple. Putting her arm around the slightly older woman's waist, she hugged her. "We are all grief stricken. It happened so suddenly," She said, and ended on a sob.

Sylvia pushed the two away, disconnecting herself and glared at the two adults.

"Why are you here? Go home. You aren't needed or wanted. I will mourn my loss alone, thank you very much." Her voice screeched.

"Sylvia." Countered the son, who looked her in the eyes. "We stayed in the back of the crowd and didn't announce our presence. I thought it best to let you show your sorrow to the town and not interrupt the service by coming to the front of the line. But now it's late, we haven't eaten and it's far too dangerous to drive back to Boston after this rain in the dark. We need to spend the night." Simon commanded.

She stared at the two couples and three children. "Fine, tell Cook you are all staying for dinner and breakfast. You can stay in your old rooms," her voice filled with sarcasm added, "the little brats can sleep with you. I'll have extra blankets sent up to make pallets on the floor."

Sylvia stormed out of the room. She needed a hot bath and dry clothing. She glanced at the grandfather clock as she stepped into the foyer. She had an hour before dinner would be served.

CHAPTER THREE

Sylvia entered the dining room, and stood before her husband's chair … at the head of the table. She sat. Glaring at the seven uninvited guests who stood upon her arrival, she nodded her head. Her step-family sat as Sylvia rang the silver bell beside her plate.

The soup arrived. Picking up her spoon, she began eating without offering a blessing over the meal. The adults and their children bowed their heads for a moment before they began to eat in silence. Sylvia required no conversation. The well behaved children were spaced between their parents. No one spoke as Sylvia watched the interlopers with squinted eyes. *They invade my privacy and eat my food. What will they do next to disrupt my evening?*

All at the table remained silent as the main course was served. She watched as the adults kept their heads down, looking at their food as though it was a piece of priceless art. She noticed the little maggots had finally stopped looking up at her and smiling. When dessert arrived, the children licked their lips as the apple pie with ice cream was placed before them.

Simon placed his fork on the empty plate. "Thank you for allowing us to stay the night, Sylvia. I do have one last favor to ask, provided it won't be too much trouble."

He took a deep breath, "Sylvia, we were wondering if we could take a few keepsakes home to remember Father?"

Sylvia's eyes widened. She had yet to speak when he continued.

"I would like to have the clock in the entry and his shotgun."

In exasperation, she grunted.

Annabelle spoke up, "I would love to have a couple of the quilts my mother made and perhaps a six place-setting of the fine china used for special events."

Sylvia gave the two adults a sharp-squinty-eyed look.

"What, you can't make it for the auction so you can acquire my things honestly. You just want to take them out of my house?"

Inwardly, Sylvia smiled as her step-son stood, his face beet red, fists placed on the table as he attempted to get his temper in check by taking a few deep breaths.

"Oh, we can come to the auction if you like. Just remember, we were born and raised here. The people of this town watched us grow up and are our friends. Despite the pleasant face you show the people ... the foundry workers know what you really are, and that means the town also knows. Think about it, Sylvia. Who will bid against us?" His knuckles pushed further into the dining table, "If you are this greedy, I promise to bid a nickel for each lot." His voice was barely above a whisper.

He held out his hand to his wife to help her stand. "Oh, and I will pay you in pennies." He said, as he guided his wife and son from the room.

Annabelle stood, her eyes blinking in an attempt to hold back the tears threatening to run down her face. "This goes for me, too," she said, and stepped away from the table. She turned back watch Sylvia. "The only difference is I will offer a penny because you don't deserve a nickel."

Sylvia glared at her two step-children. Sparks leap from her eyes. Jaws tight she snarled, "Fine, take what you want, but I want a list and mind you I will check each item as it goes out the door."

Annabelle's husband collected their children and followed her up the stairs. Sobbing could be heard as the families climbed the stairs to their rooms.

Sylvia sat alone sipping her coffee. The evening had been full of surprises. She had no idea either of Harold's children had a backbone. They were of the age of majority when she moved in and the children moved out of the mansion soon after her arrival. At Harold's insistence, the children attended their wedding as his father's best man and her maid of honor. They had not visited since the then, and they never wrote to their father unless they sent him letters to the foundry. They only returned for the funeral. Considering the day's events, she wondered who informed them of Harold's death. If she discovered who sent word, she would destroy their entire family.

All things considered, she decided it would be worth the cost to lose a few items to keep them from attending the auction. The last thing she wanted was for them to show up and make her appear foolish.

"Yes, there will be one more surprise today, but not for me." She said, voice full of venom. "I will have one stipulation. Anything they want has to go with them tomorrow."

CHAPTER
FOUR

Sylvia returned to her room filled with the sweet taste of vengeance. She had outsmarted Harold's greedy brats and would be rid of them come morning. The auction would be delayed until she had all the money from the foundry sale, and last but not least, she would transfer the cash assets to various banks around the country. By the time the auction took place, everything will be sold, and she would be long gone.

She rang for Herman. Moments later he knocked softly. Opening her door, she handed him two notes. "Present one of these to each of the children." She instructed. "There will be no reason to wait for a response." She shut the door.

She sat in her rocker, as she did every night, trying to figure out a way to get out of town and somehow not lose the wealth she so desperately desired.

"I may have to stay here, but there isn't anything that says I can't visit family and friends for weeks at a time." She said. "Yes, with a family emergency, I can't say how long I will be gone. I will return when my family doesn't need me. As for visiting that dreadful grave … the dead must wait for the living."

Smiling to herself, she climbed into bed. *I've won, and they didn't even know there was a game.* She snuggled herself into the soft mattress and warm blankets and fell asleep.

Herman arrived at Simon's door and rapped twice. The conversation behind the door ceased, and Simon slowly opened the door, blocking the opening. He tilted his head at Herman and wondered what the manservant wanted.

He handed one of the two pieces of paper to Simon.

Herman stepped to the other bedroom door. He started to rap, but hesitated. He looked back at Simon and said, "Your father was a good man and a gentleman. He treated everyone with respect and kindness. Madam is not that type of person."

He paused, then continued, "Before you ask, I

remain for lack of anywhere to go. At my age, no one will hire me. She knows my situation and extends her abuse in many ways. Please, always be kind to those who serve you."

He knocked on the second door.

"Herman." Simon said, before the door was opened, "If this becomes too much, join me at my home, you will always be welcome. If you wish, you may continue to serve the family you love."

"Thank you, sir. But Madam will have no one to assist her if I leave." He sighed, "She is your father's wife. I am obligated to care for her, in respect for your father's memory."

Annabelle accepted the note and thanked Herman as he turned to return to the main floor. He stopped and bowed to both of the children.

"Sir, Madam, it was an honor to assist in your growing up. You are kind and respectable people." He said and walked away.

The four adults were sitting in Simon's room discussing Sylvia's order to take whatever they wanted, but what was left when they walked out the door would remain in the house.

Annabelle crumbled the note. "How can she be so cruel? She knows we can't take the things we want. There is no room in our cars."

"Seems appropriate for Sylvia," Simon commented. "We have to be out in the morning. We don't have time to pack and ship everything to Boston by train."

The room was silent and the four adults considered their options. Simon stood and looked out the window, thinking.

"Annabelle, do you remember Ben Hastings?"

She thought for a minute, "Yes, big strong man that protected me from a couple of drunks who tried to drag me into an alley when I was fifteen. Why?"

Simon smiled and walked into the hall. "He's a hauler here in town. He's got the manpower and wagons to move anything we choose."

He picked up the hall phone. "Hello Ruby, yes it's Simon. Good to hear your voice, yes it has been years. Listen, could you connect me with Ben Hastings, I have a bit of a problem and I'm hoping he can help me."

Moments later, the phone rang at the other end of the line and the ever friendly voice of an old time friend answered. "Hello Ben, this is Simon Davlen. Yes, it was a beautiful service. He left us so fast, there were so many things I wanted to tell him. But I will talk to him from that quiet place in my heart."

He took a deep breath as he continued, "I know this is short order, but I was wondering if you have a couple of wagons available tomorrow morning. Annabelle and

I have some things we want to take back to Boston."

There was silence while Simon listened to Ben's response.

"Yes, it must be in the morning. You know there is no love-loss between Sylvia, Anabelle and myself. Everything must go with us in the morning, or we will have no physical memories of our lives with our parents."

Cheryl, Simon's wife sat quiet as she listened. Annabelle was waiting her turn with the list the two of them had made since supper.   "Great, Ben, this is a life saver. My biggest item is the Grandfather clock in the entryway, my roll top desk, a couple of quilts, Dad's shotguns and some furniture. Let me put Annabelle on the phone with her list. If the driver doesn't mind spending an extra day out of town, I think it can all go in one wagon … Great thanks. Here's my sister."

"Oh, Ben, if there is extra room, can we add more memories." Simon paused, "Great, that's a big wagon. I think we will add beds and dressers, just to fill the empty spots in our house."

Annabelle took the receiver and thanked him again for his kindness when she was young. She chatted with him for a few minutes, asked about his family and all the other things that are important to a woman.

"My list is similar to Simon's only I want things like quilts, and homemade treasures." She paused. "Oh that much room. That's great, I will add my bedroom furniture as well. Thank you, Ben. Once again you have come to my rescue."

CHAPTER
FIVE

Sylvia enjoyed her morning coffee as her visitors joined her at the table. She smiled, "I hope you have your list to make sure you take everything with you when you go. Otherwise you will be informed of the auction and you can bid with your spare change."

Everyone took their seats in silence. Simon poured himself some coffee and handed the carafe to his wife. He took a sip and grinned at his step mother. "I thought you might have a little trick up your sleeve, especially when I mentioned the clock." His smile grew from ear to ear, "I called Ben Hastings and he will be here in half an hour with a furniture wagon to take everything to Boston."

He handed two sheets of paper to his stepmother. "This is what we will be taking. We aren't greedy, but we do want our memories. The items at the end of the lists are only if there is room to pack them."

Sylvia opened the folded papers. Her jaw dropped as she read the list. But she covered the action by raising her coffee cup to her lips. Surprised at how little the two wanted, she decided it wasn't worth the energy to fight. "Fine. Get loaded and get out," she said tapping her finger on the papers. "If you want to go to the grave get it done this morning, I will be going up after lunch, and I don't want to see your faces again."

The seven ate. Sylvia exchanged hateful glances at her step-children while Simon held a smug look of victory.

Herman stepped into the room and addressed Simon. "Sir, Mr. Hastings is here to see you."

Simon rose and left the room.

CHAPTER SIX

Mid-afternoon, Sylvia arrived at the gates of the cemetery. Taking a deep breath, she sauntered to the grave and greeted other people making their way along the sidewalk.

She stood at the headstone, looking down, she turned her head and scanned the grounds, noting where individuals and families visited lost loved ones. Harold was in one of the last family plots, high on the hill. She spotted Tim Wilkerson, talking to his wife several yards down and to her left, Tamm Whitecliff sat with her two children on a bench halfway down the hill, and the remaining visitors were down below where the newly buried rotted in the ground. She didn't want someone sneaking up on her and consider her crazy for talking out loud to her invisible tormentor.

"Well, you old son of a bitch, your kids came and spent the night at my house. Your spawn robbed me blind by taking my things for themselves. The good news is they are gone forever. Your dried up soul won't find any pleasure in their future visits."

Thanks to the veil covering her face, no one could see her eyes slit like a cobra as she spewed her pent-up-venom over the grave. The deep bass voice entered her head, "Ah, Sylvia. The poor man is dead, feeding the worms. Can you not show a bit of kindness to his memory and his children?"

She grabbed the side of her head with her hands and shook it. "Get out of my head specter. Its daylight, the sun is shining, and you … you should not be able to torment me." She commanded. In anger she stomped her foot at the edge of the head stone with such force that it moved, splattering her shoes with mud. "Be Gone."

"Calm down, my dear or you will have a heart attack. It would be a shame to die before your time. You must live so you don't miss out on the changes and excitement about to enter your life."

Sylvia looked in the direction of the voice. She had questions … what changes and excitement? I have everything planned to the last detail.

"Besides," he continued, "I am no specter, ghost, or even your poor dead husband's consciousness. I am something of a friend, although this is the first occasion for us to meet." That deep boulders rolling laugh seemed to echo on the cemetery grounds. "I have known you since you were a young girl. You were special then and now you are unique. You have kept my attention all these years."

Sylvia scanned the grounds once again to see if anyone heard him. No one looked her way.

"Don't worry, my dear. Only you can hear me." The voice whispered. "I know your past, your present and your future my dear. I am your only true friend."

Sylvia stepped away from the head stone. "I really don't care what you think you know. You aren't my friend … You are a gobemouche trying to interfere in my business. You aren't real."

Sylvia paused. She looked toward the sound of the voice and spit," You are nothing more than my imagination. Besides, I'm going on a trip where you can't follow me as I travel the world because you are stuck here, in this land of the dead."

Her invisible tormentor laughed. "Oh Sylvia, I'm not stranded in the land of the dead. I can leave anytime I wish, but I gain strength among the visitors coming here. I am learning your personality. In all the earth, you have become my favorite. I find you adorable. One day we will meet on equal terms, and then the true fun will begin."

With a grunt, she turned and slowly walked to the gate, head down. She ignored everyone on the path, bumping into people who did not notice her inattention to her surroundings.

"Don't plan that trip too soon." The voice taunted in her head. "There is a will to be read in a few weeks. You might want to be present to see what you get out of poor Harold."

The widow stopped. "Continue" she whispered.

"Oh...he made a new will before passing." The voice quipped in a sing song manner. "It has been verified by the state court. You might want to be there to defend your wealth."

Sylvia huffed. "Well, I can hold off on my trip. I guess we will talk again tomorrow?"

"Most definitely, and every day you remain here."

Sylvia nodded. "My albatross."

"Alas, I must say good bye. We are at the cross roads, and I wish to go no farther ... for now."

Sylvia felt a chill run through her body as she sensed a hand on her shoulder. She turned to see who had touched her, but there was no one near her. Shaking her head, she continued her journey to the front gate.

She considered all the new information her

"Albatross" had given her as she rode home in the carriage. There is a new will, forcing her to change her plans to leave this filthy god forsaken place.

CHAPTER
SEVEN

Sylvia stood at the graveside. "I've visited you for the past forty-days. Didn't matter if it was raining, sunny or snow was falling on the ground. For forty-days you have told me things about my past, hinted about my future. All you have done is give headaches day after day." She spat. "Yet, I have grown accustomed to your deep voice. You have made me proud of my accomplishments."

'Spector' as she named her new companion continued her biography on their next meeting and every day she paid a visit to the grave.

Thinking back to the second week, "Your smooth

voice made me remember how proud I was when I killed my two brothers and sister without one bit of suspicion falling on my head." She whispered out loud.

At the age of thirteen, she burned down the house, as her parents slept in their bed thanks to a large dose of laudanum added to their evening wine. Sylvia felt bad that they slept through the fire, because she wanted to hear their screams.

She was now accustomed to his telling of her victories over competition for lovers, enemies who tried to keep her from gaining favor with employers. It gave her the feeling that she was a great angel of vengeance in an unforgiving world.

As was his habit, her 'friend' left her at the walkway by the grave. Giving a dismissive wave of her hand, she made her way to the carriage and home. Today, she didn't feel the pot holes and bumps in the road. Her thoughts, refocused on the planning and execution of her first human kills. She smiled, the true smile of someone reliving a happy memory.

"Let me see," he paused, "After a few weeks in your first foster home, the pet dog disappeared and a month later their baby died in its sleep. The family suspected you rolled the baby on a thick feather pillow, face down. The dog was never found and they assumed you did something to it too. They returned you to the system."

He paused as though looking over the grounds. "The next few months in the orphanage taught you many skills

... how to steal, hide things in plain sight and to set up your fellow orphans to take the blame for something you did. After four months, a relative was discovered and you were delivered to your thirty year old aunt. Quite the teacher in the ways of grown-ups wasn't she."

Sylvia looked toward the voice, a snarl on her face. "Aunt Lulabelle forced me to learn the sexual ways of men and woman. We belonged to anyone with the right price for thirty minutes. There were four of us, I was the oldest and barely a teen. I grew up fast after I joined the house. Day and night customers would come, and we had to present ourselves in the living room, barely dressed and forced strut our young bodies."

Her hands became fists as she remembered the abuse. "The customers would choose one or two of the girls. Sometimes it would be a couple, or two of the same sex, but it was always the same result. The chosen were escorted to a room where the 'young ladies' would provide relaxation and entertainment for the adults."

Spector whispered into her ear, "Your aunt collected all the money. She refused to give you young girls anything ... said it was for lodging and food."

"Ah, but you were the smart one. You quietly watched her, and when it was to your advantage, you knew where she kept the money, the safe hidden behind the big picture in her office. In time you saw where she the key to open the giant treasure chest was kept."

Sylvia's thoughts returned to her days in the whore

house, always looking for a way to escape, but with no money or friends she was trapped in a life she hated.

"Yes, I hated the two years I existed in that hell hole." She admitted to Specter, "Until the day one of the customers went too far in his demands."

Her feral smile returned. "It all happened so fast. The guy was big and grabbed me by the shoulders and pushed me to my knees. He was rough, told me to do the job right or he would break my jaw."

"Yes, I remember what you did," the voice said in admiration. "On your knees you pulled down his zipper and removed his equipment. Looking up at him with an innocent smile, you bit off his male parts and spit them on the floor."

Spector sighed in adoration, reliving the memory with Sylvia. "He fell to the floor, howling like a banshee as blood soaked into the cheap carpet."

Sylvia licked her lips as though tasting the blood that overflowed from her mouth when she extracted her revenge.

She reminisced with a smile and whispered, "When Lulabelle charged into the room, I took the knife strapped to his belt and cut open her lower belly, carving a large circle. She sat next to the man trying to hold her guts inside. When she lost her grip, the soft parts spread all over the floor."

"A most excellent piece of work, although messy," the voice said in admiration. "You did improve over time, learning the poisons and plants that leave no trace, even a pillow over the head of someone having had breathing problems to begin with. I was surprised at the hours and days you spent in the library studying methods to kill."

There was silence for a few moments as the two relived the adventures.

"The other girls were hiding in the linen closet. You opened the door and painted the room with their blood. It was such a beautiful mess as you stabbed and sliced them into small pieces. If I remember, you took blood from each girl and rubbed it over your naked body. You saturated the walls, floor and the white linens in their gore. You were efficient, destroying the three, slicing in ways that produced a lot of blood, but it took time for the three to bleed out and died. You studied them as their lives slipped away. It looked like you were admiring your work, or perhaps studying your technique."

Sylvia closed her eyes and watched herself celebrate the thrill of the kill after the three had gasped their last breath. She took a long hot shower, dressed and packed a small suitcase with clothes. Before leaving the house, she went to the basement and broke a gas line.

"I went back upstairs and opened the safe and stuffed all the cash from the big metal safe and the extra money from desk drawers into a large purse and lit a candle on an end table in the living room. Closing the front door, I placed a small 'closed' sign on the door knob. I was blocks away when the building blew up." She said in wistful memory.

"Fun times, huh Sylvia?" the voice said. "Training days - honing your skills – making you the woman you are today."

She glared at the sound of his voice. "You know so much about my life," sarcasm dripping as he had once again struck a nerve, "I can't wait to hear what else you know about me. We can write a book and I can be rich calling it crime fiction."

She made her way toward the exit, lost in thoughts and memories of her early 'thrill kills'. She didn't realize her invisible friend remained beside her as she walked through the main gate.

CHAPTER EIGHT

"Another day, another conversation with my invisible friend," she said leaning on the headstone. Spector had been talkative for most of the hour, then went quiet. Invisible, Sylvia looked for the shimmering of his essence, but he wasn't there.

"Come back and play." She commanded, "Tell me more of my adventures with husbands and how you know what I have done."

Most days Sylvia would let her 'walking life story' talk uninterrupted. Other days, she would add personal feelings or thoughts about a variety of kills. It was nice to have someone to talk about her past adventures. But he often upset her with his personal comments about her skills and choices of victims.

She was making her way to the main gate when the voice whispered in her ear. "I especially enjoyed you having your second husband run over by a horse and buggy, followed by a wagon. It was an inventive way to end his life with you standing right there and not a single person suspected you pushed him under the carriage."

She smiled. She remembered the thump of the horse's hooves as they punched through skin and flesh to snap the breast bone with a crack that had been music to her ears. As planned, she screamed as the second wagon rolled over his body and the front wheel ran across his mi- section, cutting the body in half. Women pulled her away from the 'accident', shielding her, preventing her from enjoying the mutilation of the body when they pulled him from under the wagon.

Sylvia stopped her travels and relived those wonderful moments. Having grown weary of poisons and plants, she planned more creative deaths. Now at the age of forty-eight she was getting too old to plan such complicated adventures. *Men look for much younger women. Even the old farts preferred a woman in their twenties.*

She was jolted back to reality when her 'friend' said. "I will see you tomorrow afternoon, my dear." His voice casual, yet filled with some kind of dark joy. "The reading of the will is tomorrow morning." He said then made that gravely sound he called a laugh "The note is waiting for you when you get home. Aren't you excited with all the surprises and new obstacles coming your way? You won't be bored for a while, my dear?"

She half turned to face him, but changed her mind and stomped away from the 'land of the dead' and took her carriage home.

CHAPTER
NINE

Arriving at the attorney's office, Sylvia took a moment to school her expression into that of the grieving widow. It required some effort to camouflage her contempt for Conrad Wadsworth. She despised the … corporate leech. He had been Harold's attorney for over five decades, handling all the old goat's business affairs.

Why hadn't he used the family attorney I hired? We have a good relationship. Giving him a little lip service, he would have told me what the old fart was doing.

She released a long breath before opening the front door. Without a word, the pinched-face secretary rose to escort Sylvia through the door to the inner office. She gave a curt nod to her boss and pulled the door closed behind her with a quiet click.

Sylvia resisted the urge to frown at the lawyer, but she could not contain the scowl from blemishing her careful countenance as she discovered Annabelle, Simon, Herman and Cook sitting in chairs a few feet from the desk.

"I thought I was rid of the two of you and your mutant children" She snapped, pointing at her step-children sitting quietly in the corner of the room.

Glancing over to her staff she grumbled, "What are you two doing here? You're hired help, at least for now."

"Mrs. Davlen," Conrad chided, without looking up from the papers he studied. "Why don't you take a seat so we can get started?"

Sylvia huffed and sat in the chair directly facing the lawyer. "All Right Mr. Wadsworth, why am I here and what is all this crap about a will? I have a copy of the will in my bag" she said reaching into her bag pulling out an oversized envelope. "Everything belongs to me." Her voice echoed off the walls.

Conrad ignored her outburst as he continued looking over the documents. After exactly one minute, he stacked the papers into a neat pile, and regarded the people in his office.

"We are here to read the most recent, and final will of Harold Davlen. As requested by the will, everyone is now present." He said.

Conrad stood, moved to the door. "Miss Hinson, please join us and bring your pad."

The secretary entered and sat in a chair behind the attorney.

"My secretary has been instructed to record your comments during the reading and any written requests afterward. All documents presented and comments will be added and become an official part of the recording of this event."

He looked at Sylvia. "In answer to your question, Mrs. Davlen, your husband approached me two years after the wedding. Certain comments did not correspond with your earlier life's stories. Mr. Davlen came to me as all business between us was and remains confidential. At his instruction, I hired a private investigator to check your background."

He paused.

Sylvia sat as stoic as a statue.

"It appears, Mrs. Davlen that until eight years ago, you did not exist. You are a ghost. Your picture was circulated through various law enforcement agencies, as well as banks and investment firms." Again he paused, "facts began to surface, and shall we say ... you have had an interesting life."

Conrad placed his left hand on a stack of papers and continued, "This will was written, signed and filed with the courts before he became ill. I want you to know, Mrs. Davlen, that he loved you with all his heart. Unfortunately, he did not follow my recommendation to divorce you. He remained married to you and instead expressed his final decisions within this document."

Looking at the other people in the room, he said, "Your father and employer loved you all and asks for your forgiveness in bringing this woman into the home. He felt his honor was tarnished and hoped this," Conrad raised the papers in a salute, "makes amends for all you have been through."

Sylvia rolled her eyes and leaned forward. "Of for god's sakes, Wadsworth, get on with it. If I want a sermon, I'll attend church."

Conrad smiled to the group and began reading the opening remarks, all the legal comments about the will, Harold being of sound mind and the like. His pace was slow and calm, giving each person the opportunity to understand and ask questions. The room remained quiet.

"Will you get on with it, I'm a busy woman and you are wasting my time" Sylvia growled.

Conrad glanced up. Taking a drink of water, he cleared his throat and continued.

"My young and beautiful wife. To me, you were heaven on earth. But, once we married the house began to empty. At this writing, only two servants remain. My son and daughter left home and began careers that did not involve the foundry. They created grandchildren I never got to meet. You had me disown them with profound arguments of their youth, success and you being alone without support when something happened to me."

Conrad looked up at Sylvia as she raised her veil. Crossing her arms, she frowned at the attorney with hate filled eyes.

"Sylvia, after finding myself without friends and you as my only family, I came to the realization you had purposefully run everyone out of my life. You became abusive in sly ways that could only come with experience. As you talked of your life, I began to notice how the stories contradicted each other. This prompted me to ask Conrad to look into your past. What he discovered was disquieting. I chose not to talk to the authorities. My health declined a bit at a time and I realized my days were numbered. Near the end, I knew I had made the right decision as my life faded far too fast to be normal. I had made this will my number one priority as well as selling the foundry prior to my death."

Sylvia's mouth opened and closed, but no sound came forth. *How long did he know her history? Why had he remained kind and loving?*

"Eventually the investigators discovered a clue and traveled out west. As your past exploits surfaced, we hired more investigators to dig even deeper. Reports came to me, detailing how you are wanted for questioning in three states, under various names, for the deaths of your previous husbands. I learned the authorities named you The Black Widow, but, still, I couldn't give you up."

Sylvia leaned forward, taking a few deep breaths. She felt the color drain from her face, she felt light headed. "Lies ... All Lies. Harold was my first and only love." She argued.

Conrad rested his arms on the desk, leaning in. "My dear, everything has been verified. This is why there is a new will. Oh, don't worry, he has taken good care of you ... with stipulations."

CHAPTER TEN

"I think it's time to read the distribution of assets. Although your past is interesting …. I will spare the others the details." Conrad's voice remained professionally disinterested. "It was a surprise to all of you, including Sylvia, to be invited to this meeting."

His eyes returned to the paper. "To my son and his wife, I leave him one-hundred-thousand dollars, and to their children, a scholarship of ten-thousand- dollars each.

To my daughter and her husband, I also leave one – hundred- thousand dollars, and to their daughter a ten-thousand-dollar scholarship."

He focused on the two couples and smiled before continuing, "If additional children are produced from your marriage, a ten-thousand-dollar scholarship will be created in their names."

Sylvia's face flushed with anger. "No," she bellowed. "He disowned them, they get nothing. I get it all, every last penny." She thrust to her feet and slammed a fist on the desk. "I won't allow this, I will contest. - I will ... I will ..." Unable to finish, she turned to her step-children. "You get nothing, do you hear me -- Nothing? I will see to it."

"Sylvia," Conrad barked. "If you contest, it will go to court and your secrets will be made public."

Sylvia collapsed in the chair, gasping for air.

Conrad called for a fifteen-minute recess. He poured a glass of water from the pitcher on his desk and set it in front of her.

When they were ready to continue, the family filed into the office as the secretary was exchanging the straight-backed chair with a soft, overstuffed chair for Sylvia. A kindness Sylvia would never have given another person.

"Let's continue." Conrad said, after everyone was

seated. "To my butler, and best friend, Herman, I bequeath fifty-thousand-dollars. To my cook, Jean Marie, I also bequeath fifty-thousand-dollars. I give my blessings to them, as they leave this town in search of a better life. You two have remained faithful to me for many years and you have no further obligations to my widow."

Conrad shuffled a few papers, "The money for these gifts has been withdrawn from a secured account and certified checks are held in their names at the bank."

The lawyer paused, lifting flat eyes to Sylvia, he continued. "As you all know, the foundry has been sold for a considerable sum."

Sylvia lifted a hand to interrupt, "I already know, I must remain here for the next eighteen months, visit his grave daily and will receive money in six month intervals. If I leave town or fail to visit the grave, I forfeit."

"That is correct Mrs. Davlen," he nodded. "but there are other details concerning the sale proceeds."

Conrad sipped his water then cleared his throat. "First, ten percent of each payment will be given to Harold's son and daughter, five percent to Herman and Jean Marie."

Sylvia gaped, but remained silent.

"Second, since you have no family, there is no need for travel. You must remain in this town and visit the grave daily … regardless of weather, as you have said, Mrs. Davlen. Next, you will support all the charities sponsored by your deceased husband. However, you may not retain a seat on any of their boards.

Regarding the foundry, itself, the new owner and manager will arrive to take control of the business mid-May. You will make room for him at the mansion, providing room and board until you have met your obligations in the next year and a half. If you have any questions or wish to deviate from these rules, you will address the situation with the executor of the estate, his decision rules. Otherwise you lose everything, house, money in the bank and the fund set up for the semi-annual deposits."

Conrad placed a hand on his chest grinning at Sylvia. "I have been granted the honor of executor."

Sylvia grimaced. "Of course, you have."

Still grinning, Conrad returned his gaze to the papers in his hand. "The executor will complete your last will and testament," he pointed a beefy finger at Sylvia, "leaving everything to Annabelle and Simon. You will sign it and it will be filed with the courts. If you attempt to create any other will, you will lose everything and your history will be released to the proper authorities. If I should die within two years of the completion of your obligations, your past will be released to the authorities. I want you to be perfectly clear in your understanding as to what will happen if you disobey this will," The lawyer concluded, his gaze bored into Sylvia.

Sylvia glared daggers at the balding dome of the sleaze bag as he sat the final paper neatly on the stack.

"Any questions or comments?" he asked, stuffing the papers into a folder and handing it to his secretary.

The family and two servants shook their heads, smiling.

Conrad returned their smiles and stood. "Very well, this concludes the reading of the will. Thank you all for coming in."

Rounding his desk, he went to the door and shook hands with each person as they left. His secretary continued to sit in her chair, pad and pen at the ready.

Sylvia remained in her chair staring at her hands. "I will have my family lawyer review ALL the paperwork." she said.

Returning to his desk, Conrad shrugged, "I could send copies to him this afternoon." He opened a drawer and produced a thick, legal-sized envelope. "Or, if you prefer, you can take this packet, review the will and the findings of the investigation with him. Be aware, your family lawyer isn't very good at keeping secrets. If he talks about your past lives, you will end up being arrested and lose everything."

The attorney handed the envelope to Sylvia. "I will let you decide if you want to give this to your attorney.

Everything here is a certified copy. The originals are in a safe place."

Sylvia snatched the packet out of Conrad's hands and crumpled it against her chest. "I will review this and give him what I feel is necessary."

Conrad stood as Sylvia began to rise.

"Let me remind you, Mrs. Davlen, "If anything happens to me in the next four years, your secret is out." He stood and held out his hand, "Have a good day, madam."

Sylvia looked at his hand but did not reach out to take it. "I'm still a rich woman, I will hire new servants, maintain the house, and live my life as directed."

Head held high, chin thrust out, she walked out the door and headed to the cemetery. *I might as well go and spit on his grave. Hell, if no one is there, I may just piss on it as well.*

CHAPTER ELEVEN

As she entered the gates she made a mental note to wire the city for new hired help. In addition, a new bedroom set for her boarder, all new bedding, towels and necessities to make the home respectable. After the amount of work required to clean and serve the home, six servants should suffice. Nothing was too good for her new master.

Sylvia saw the shimmering of her specter sitting on the head stone long before she reached the grave. *Humph, he's waiting to gloat, the bastard.*

She halted at the foot of the grave as his shimmering

figure slid off the granite block.

"Well, are you a rich woman once again, Sylvia?"

"Not as rich as I should be. But I guess I have to live with it. How long have you known about all this?"

Laughing, he said, "Who do you think put the thought of checking your background in your late husband's head?"

Her jaw dropped and a whoosh of air escaped, as if she'd been punched in the breadbasket. What was this creature that he could interfere with her life so?

Anger oozed from within her. She snapped her jaw shut and glared at the misty being.

"How dare you. I'm stuck in this dump for eighteen months. A year and a half, and I have to visit this grave every day where I'm sure you'll be waiting to continue tormenting me with a recounting of my miserable past. To laugh at the life I was forced to live."

"Oh, my dear Sylvia, you have money safely banked, with an allowance to operate the house. When it's all over, you will actually have more money than you can spend when you kick the mud off your shoes the day you leave." He floated close to her, and brushed his mouth against her ear, "Besides, you never know, a new adventure may turn up when you least expect it."

Sylvia growled and marched toward the gate. The ghostly being accompanied her. Though she pretended to ignore him, she always listened closely, just in case he said something useful.

"Tell me Sylvia, why did you have husband number four fall from the roof of a ten story building? He could barely walk, even with two canes. You brought him the edge and sat him on the ledge." Spector Asked.

Sylvia smiled at the memory. "Yes, the man could barely walk, but always wanted me to ease his tension. I pulled down his pants, sat him down, raised my dress and started to sit on his lab. Instead, I used my back side to push him over. I gave him quite a final thrill."

"You certainly caught him by surprise ... so surprised he didn't even scream on the way down." He finished.

"Yes, the escape took planning. I ran down two flights of stairs, went around the hall and down two more flights of stairs. I waited for the elevator to go up to the top floor, hit the 'down' button, and made my escape as they climbed the stairs to the roof." She sighed from the memory. "I exited the building in time to see the old perverts body flattened on the sidewalk."

The apparition's voice waivered with delight as he complimented her on the imaginative way she had finished off Mr. McIntosh.

Sylvia continued to smile as she exited through the front gate. It wasn't until she sat in front of the fire that evening, enjoying a cup of tea, when she realized the spook had been standing on the curb as her carriage pulled away. She noticed how his essence floated apart then returned to his body when people walked through him.

CHAPTER
TWELVE

Sylvia wasted no time putting the new staff to work cleaning the entire house and assigning daily chores for each individual. The upstairs bedroom was scrubbed clean and the rest of the house was cleaned from top to bottom in preparation for its new resident.

Five days later, the new furniture arrived. The delivery men assembled the bed and placed the remaining furniture as directed.

She saw to it that only the best foods were delivered to fill the pantry and refrigerator.

Upon sending a note to Conrad that she required extra money to pay for the increased expenses of preparing the house for its new master, Sylvia was summoned to the attorney's office.

She bypassed the secretary and marched into Conrad's office with a scowl on her face and clinched fists.

"Summoned. I've been summoned to your office. Who gave you the authority to summon me and just what do you want?"

The attorney pulled his eyes away from the document he was reading and smiled. "Thank you for dropping by Mrs. Davlen." He laid the paper aside and indicated one of the facing chairs. "Won't you have a seat?"

"I prefer to stand as I won't be here long."

"Very well," he said, reclaiming the document and raking his eyes over the contents. "We need to discuss your recent expenses. You are far over budget and we haven't reached mid-month. And for the record, your husband's will gives me the authorization to summon you to my office."

Glaring at the pompous ass, Sylvia dropped into one of the chairs. The legs grated on the hardwood floor as she scooted the chair forward. She swiped a hand across the polished wood desktop, scattering neat stacks of documents across the floor.

She leaned her arms on the desk and folded her fingers together. "With having to hire servants, purchase new furniture for the bedroom, and stock the kitchen, I would have assumed that even a shyster like yourself would realize the first month would be over budget."

Ignoring the mess, Conrad removed a folder from his center drawer, fingering through the sheets he pulled out a sheet and said, "Did you have to get your staff from one of the top homemaker agencies in New York? The rates are three times the price from other agencies in this area."

Sylvia was beginning to enjoy this argument. "The way I see it, I have six young, healthy individuals that can work in shifts, keep the entire house presentable and have the ability to provide adequate service should the new foundry manager want to entertain. These folks are top of the line and have already upgraded the interior of the house with their cleaning abilities."

Conrad tapped a finger on the folder. "I have an invoice here for over six-thousand dollars for bedroom furniture. This is unreasonable."

"Well Conrad, what did you expect? Those leeches for step-children emptied both bedrooms. I had to buy all new furniture for my new boarder. I bought the good stuff that lasts. He should be impressed with the way his room looks." She paused and decided to twist the knife. "If I am ordered to accept another boarder, expect another bill for furniture."

"Why not simply prepare your husband's old room?"

Sylvia scoffed, "The hospital reclaimed the bed as soon as they took the body. The furniture was old and in disrepair." She waved a hand in front of her nose. "The smell of sickness and death. Unfortunately, the excellent cleaning skills of my help could not eliminate all the odors." Sylvia gave an exaggerated sigh. "It will need to be stripped and renovated before anyone can stay in it."

She smiled at Conrad's nod. Even he could not argue with her logic.

With a frown, he said, "One last question. Did you have to buy seven sets of sheets, blankets, six pillows and a dozen pillow covers for one man?"

Sylvia smirked. "Yes. The other linens were old and thin. The beds require changing daily since the grime from the foundry soils the bedding. I needed decent sheets as well plus one extra set should weather prevent any washing.- Don't worry, you penny pinching shark, I won't buy more furniture or bedding until it becomes necessary."

The attorney thumbed through several other papers, "I have totaled all your receipts for food, supplies, sanitary items and a variety of miscellaneous products. Care to explain the purpose of all these items?"

He placed the receipts in front of her.

Sylvia ground her teeth. "Are you really this stupid? It takes more to run the household now. I have gone from meager meals for three people and a dying man to seven

58

healthy people with an eighth on the way. Everything is stocked, but I will have to order fresh food every week. You need to adjust the budget. Get used to it." She told him. "The incidentals are necessary in every home."

Conrad glowered at her. "Your pantry is stocked. Keep it that way. I will adjust it when Mr. Mot arrives. But, that is the only adjustment I will consider. In all other aspects, you will stay within budget or you will have to compensate with staff."

Sylvia stood. "I hope you don't intend to starve everyone out of the house. If things get lean, I'm sure the new foundry owner will pay you a visit and set you straight."

Pushing the chair back with her legs, it tilted onto the rear legs and fell to the floor with a clatter as she stormed out of his office.

CHAPTER
THIRTEEN

Sylvia found herself anticipating her daily visits to the cemetery. It wasn't that she enjoyed her conversations with Spector, but his appreciation for her artistic endeavors in murder rubbed away a little of her resentment of her current situation. It was unseemly, but she felt he understood her--and stood by her.

"Spring is just around the corner, Sylvia. The new owner will arrive soon. Be pleasant. He wields more power than you think."

Baring her teeth into her famous smile, she said, "Oh I will be kind, pleasant and attentive. After all, he is rich and owns my foundry. I will convince him I would be an excellent partner."

The two strolled around the empty cemetery.

"Ah Sylvia, already plotting your next conquest, and you haven't left town." Spector crooned.

"Don't be a fool, you invisible fiend," she chuckled. "I merely suggest a partnership with me would be advantageous." She shrugged. "After all, I am the previous owner's widow. Who better to advise him in the running of the foundry and to help him gain acceptance in the town?"

She looked into the shimmering light, where his eyes should be, and said, "What do you know about him?"

"He has an interesting name. But, that's not what you want to know so it isn't important. What have you gleaned from your conversations with the lawyer?"

"Not much. The shyster said everything was handled by his lawyer and paperwork was sent back and forth by currier. His arrival has been delayed twice, but Conrad said he should arrive soon. The house is ready and he will be welcomed like a member of the family."

Spector laughed, "Yes, family. I know what you have done to your family."

The two returned to the gravesite. Though the grounds keepers kept the site neat and clean, there were no fresh flowers by the headstone and Harold was otherwise forgotten.

She stared at Harold's grave. "You sneaky bastard. Everything should have been mine. You may have won this battle, but you will lose the war." She leaned in close to the headstone. "I'll get my hands on the foundry and shut it down. No more money to your greedy children. I will turn this place a ghost town.

She spit on the grave.

Spector walked beside her as she headed for the front gate. Lost in thought, Sylvia walked along the outside wall until she spotted a carriage to take her home. She didn't look around or would have felt her invisible friend standing behind her."

Spector watched her ride away. He wondered why she always selected a public horse and buggy instead of the more comfortable automobiles.

Well, time to pay a visit to the hospital and nursing home and see who is tired of sickness, pain and torment. I will offer them peace. They will call me an angel and I will collect their souls.

Gliding along the sidewalk he laughed to himself. *I was never held captive in the cemetery. But allowed her to assume I was confined. Now she almost trusts me and doesn't pay attention to me. She listens to me as I feed her bits and pieces of information, patting her back as I help her relive all her conquests...all the deaths.*

I am more than a reaper, I am more than the grim reaper. I have the power to not only choose where and when but how souls leave the body. My reapers simply collect the souls that are scheduled for death. My second cleaves the souls of those descending to the pits. As for myself, I am the boss and choose who I want to play with before claiming them. Good, bad, or just interesting people...those belong to me.

CHAPTER FOURTEEN

The cab pulled away from the curb as he stood on the stoop, his three large suitcases beside him. The man raised his fist to the heavy, oak door and knocked, strong and loud.

A young man, tall, thin, and well dressed, opened the door. "Yes?"

"Good afternoon, sir. I am Erich Mot, the new owner of the foundry, I seek an audience with the Widow Davlen."

The butler bowed, "Good afternoon, Mr. Mot. I am James, the butler." He said, opening the door fully.

"Please come in. The mistress has been expecting you."

Entering the foyer, Erich's attention snagged on two men standing at the bottom of the stairs, as he removed his coat and hat James turned to them, issuing orders "Owen, William … there are cases to be taken to the guest bedroom."

Claiming the garments, James handed them off to Owen making no mention of the gloves Erich still wore. Leading the way down the hall, the butler slid open two pocket doors. "If you will be so kind to wait here," he said, waving a hand at the interior. "I will tell the mistress you have arrived."

Erich stepped through the doorway and ambled about the comfortable room to stretch the kinks from his long legs. Carriages were not designed for the tall statured. Several minutes later, he lowered himself onto the worn upholstery of the sofa.

He did not have to wait long before his hostess appeared in the doorway with the butler hovering behind her left shoulder.

"Good afternoon Mr. Mot. I'm Sylvia Davlen, and it is an honor to have you here." She said with a slight curtsy.

Standing, Erich studied her movements. She was very stiff and held her anger at bay by his invasion. Smiling, he bowed.

Sylvia dipped her head and moved to one of the chairs opposite him.

As she took her seat, she waved a hand at the sofa. "Please, make yourself comfortable."

"Thank you," Erich said, as he pulled the tails of his jacket toward his hips and returned to his sofa.

"Would you care for some tea, Mr. Mot?" Without waiting for his response, Sylvia nodded to the butler, who immediately left the room.

He smiled, "No need to stand on ceremony. Please, call me Erich."

"Very well, but only if you'll call me Sylvia."

"Sylvia," Erich nodded.

"I hope you find my home comfortable during your stay."

"I'm sure I will."

"I'm sure you are aware I'm recently widowed. I learned of your arrival at the reading of the will."

"I apologize for any inconvenience. I waited as long as I dare."

The pleasantries lagged as James wheeled in the tea cart and poured out. "Dinner will be served in an hour. You have time to freshen up sir. When you are ready, I will show you to your room."

Erich took his cup and caught Sylvia staring at his hands.

"I hope you don't mind my gloves. I have a skin condition. It isn't contagious, but it is not pretty to look at."

Sylvia blinked. "Not at all, they are flesh colored and I didn't notice them until now. I hope the condition is painless."

"Yes, it is a malady that has been handed down for generations. My father says it is an ancient curse. As for me, it's nothing."

Sylvia sipped her tea then changed the subject. "Where are you from, Erich?"

"My mother's people were from the north eastern shores of Europe. My father's people are from the Middle East. I am a mixture of two very strong families."

Erich thought his ears would bleed from boredom as the conversation drooled on with politeness.

When James stepped to the doorway, Erich quickly excused himself and followed the servant up the stairs. He was not looking forward to dinner. He might choke on all the civility and formality.

Nor had he anticipated all the extra people in the

house. He understood there to be just the cook and the old butler. Sylvia really had been busy. He would have to adjust his plans.

Erich nearly collided with the butler when he suddenly stopped and opened a door to the right.

"This is your room, sir. The bath is the door at the end, sir." James pointed down the path they had traveled. "There are fresh towels and there is a nice deep tub filled with hot water for your comfort. The other two bedrooms are empty, so you will have plenty of privacy."

The butler left him standing at the threshold and returned downstairs. Erich's brow furrowed as he entered the room, closing the door behind him.

CHAPTER
FIFTEEN

Dinner was quiet, with each watching the other.

Erich knew she was sizing him up as her next mark. He didn't mind. Let her enjoy her scheming. His strategy was already in play.

Sylvia placed a hand on his forearm, a gleam of mischief flashing in her eyes. "I took the liberty of announcing your arrival and have invited the acting plant manager and supervisors for breakfast. I thought your first meeting would be more pleasant in a less formal setting."

Erich smiled, "Excellent idea. We can avoid interruptions, and I can observe the men away from the plant to get a better measure of them."

"Oh, I'm so relieved," Sylvia said, touching her fingers to her chest. "I was a little concerned you might think me too presumptuous."

"Not at all. It's the kind of thinking I would expect from my wife."

Sylvia choked.

"If I had a wife," Erich said.

"I see," Sylvia recovered. "Shall we relax in the sitting room?"

"Fine."

They sipped at their sherry in silence. Occasionally, Erich shifted his eyes to Sylvia to find her staring vacantly into the fire. He imagined the wheels turning in her head. When she abruptly rose from her chair, he kept his eyes forward.

"Well, Erich, it is my bed time. Stay up as long as you like." Setting her glass on the coffee table, she left the room.

The new master of the house, sat for another hour contemplating the days ahead.

CHAPTER
SIXTEEN

Erich greeted the acting plant manager, Frank Wallace, at the door with Sylvia by his side. To Frank's credit, when Erich offered him a gloved hand, Frank clasped it firmly without a second glance.

One by one the men arrived and were introduced to their new boss. George Perry, day shift supervisor, Claude Roland and Russel Longhorn, second and third shift supervisor respectively with Archie Meeks rounding out the management team as the "floater" when various men took a day off or the workload was excessive.

They congregated at the dining room table, with Sylvia pretending to keep busy serving coffee and seeing to breakfast. Erich was aware of her every move as he listened to the men's reports.

"We have five contracts going through the plant at this very moment. Construction steel for two bridges and three buildings, as well as other contracts that are signed and waiting to begin," Frank said. "I've been communicating with various developers and steel providers. We are also in the final selection process for sheet iron to be used for military purposes."

Erich smiled and nodded, as he tracked Sylvia's movements. She caught him by surprise when she came up behind him and leaned over to refill his cup, her breasts made contact with his shoulder.

When breakfast was served, the conversation turned to family matters. Erich made mental notes about the men's home lives and their habits as they talked among themselves. He never knew what little tidbit would come in useful in the future.

As their bellies filled, the men quieted. Unable to glean any more information, it was time to move this along.

"Well gentlemen, we have had a wonderful breakfast served by a lovely hostess, but the foundry is not going to run itself." Erich said.

Standing in unison everyone thanked Sylvia for a

wonderful breakfast and allowing them to meet the new owner outside the foundry. Though they gave their compliments, none of the men smiled when speaking to her.

Erich accepted a ride to the plant from Frank, who remained silent during the short ride to the foundry. Erich allowed him the reprieve.

Once they reached the parking lot, Frank seemed to relax. They walked across the lot and Frank asked, "Would you like to tour the plant or see your office first?"

"I believe I'd like to see the plant. I've always preferred a hands-on approach."

Frank grinned. "I'm the same." He pointed with his chin. "This way."

The first day of work was underway.

CHAPTER SEVENTEEN

Days turned into weeks, and weeks turned into months. Summoned once again to Conrad's office Sylvia vowed to keep her temper and 'play nice'. She had made little progress with trying to woo Erich Mot, but she wasn't giving up.

She remembered bringing Erich to Conrad's soon after his arrival. The two became fast business friends, and Sylvia was upset when she was dismissed while they talked business.

As far as she knew, they had not talked since that first visit. But, she decided caution was the wisest course.

The secretary escorted her in, offered coffee and closed the door behind her.

Sylvia and the lawyer squared off again by staring at each other, each waiting for the other to speak first. She blew out a breath and finely gave in. "What can I do for you Conrad? I believe I am staying in budget, and I have not caused any problems. I visit the grave and attend organization meetings. So," she paused, "how may I be of service to you?"

"First of all, your payment for the foundry is ready for you to pick up at the bank. You can wire it elsewhere or keep it there." The lawyer said. "In addition, Mr. Mot is enjoying his stay at your home. He has commented several times that you are a wonderful hostess and he is quite impressed."

Sylvia felt her face turn pink. "I am honored that he is enjoying his stay. I have tried to make him comfortable. He is courteous by arriving home in time to clean up and have supper. Sometimes we sit and talk, other times he is reviewing progress reports. We have a pleasant relationship."

"Mr. Mot also commented that if he didn't know better, you are flirting with him." he said, "But I told him that it wasn't possible as you are still a grieving widow."

"Don't worry, Conrad, I'm just trying to make him feel welcome and at home while he is here," she said in a soft voice. "After all, he must return to his main office one of these days."

"I know, and I would rather you not accompany him. I know what happens to the men you marry," he said.

Sylvia looked at him wide-eyed and made an exaggerated show of offense. "Well I never... you treat a guest, a forced guest, I might add with respect, make him comfortable and this is the thanks I get for my efforts."

Red-faced, she muttered, "If there is nothing else, I will take my leave and visit the cemetery."

Conrad smiled and nodded his head, "That's about it Mrs. Davlen. Money is there when you want it. Keep Mr. Mot happy, sleep with him if you must, but don't kill him." His chuckle echoed in her ears as she stormed out the door.

"Well Spector, I got another foundry payment. Only six-months left on this prison sentence and I am rid of you and this town," she announced, walking up to the grave. "I want you to know that I have treated the new owner so well he told Conrad I was flirting with him."

"I thought you were weaving your web like the black widow you are. It's your nature."

Sylvia grunted. "Well, I may be trying to get his attention. But I certainly wouldn't bed him, like Conrad suggested. At least until we reach some kind of relationship agreement." She paused, "And there is that skin condition. If it covers his body, I may have second thoughts."

Her invisible heckler laughed. "Oh Sylvia, you would bed a syphilitic camel herder with leprosy for the right amount of money. If you want the foundry bad enough you would let him plow you like a field of cotton."

Her face grew hot. After a few seconds, she relaxed, her anger gone as fast as it hit her. "You know, you are probably right. I know I'm deranged, and it isn't the sex … it's the control … I have over powerful men."

"You have had great success over the younger and less powerful as well." Spector said. "Remember the stud in Cincinnati. You put him in a coma."

Sylvia expelled a quiet laugh. "Yes. He bragged about his size and stamina, I took him up on his offer. He wore out half-way through the night, but I continued to work him up until dawn. The stroke was an added bonus and made the night worthwhile."

"Those were the days," Spector sighed, remembering the power she held over men and some women. "Between killing and mating, there was never a dull minute in your life. I will miss those times."

Her head snapped in his direction, "And just what do you mean by that comment?"

"What I mean, Sylvia, is that you are nearing fifty,

your beauty is fading. In a few more years, you won't be able to attach yourself to a mark. You will become slow, forgetful and get caught. One day, I will need a new murderess to foster and guide."

Sylvia stared toward the creature's voice, then nodded in resignation. "You have a point. I have enough money to live like a queen the rest of my life. I will miss the hunt." She took a deep breath. "So, I will have one last fling and call it quits. I can fade away, forgotten by families and police."

"So, you will set your sites on Mot, get the foundry back and retire?"

Sylvia considered the prospect. "No, I will flirt with him, let him think he can have this well-toned and 'young' body, as he sees me. When he is hooked, I will convince him to give me half ownership of the foundry." She ran her finger over her lips, "Yes, one last challenge. One last blood bath, before I retire."

Spector chuckled. "Time for you to get home, Sylvia, and continue to weave your web."

Sylvia smiled. Since Mr. Mot ignored her usual techniques, she would have to intensify her strategies.

CHAPTER
EIGHTEEN

It had been two months since Sylva's meeting with Conrad when she was informed about Erich's leaving. To date, he had said nothing. Of course, he arrived unannounced, so one day he may just walk out the door with his suit cases. How much time before she is forced to seduce the old bore? Her thoughts flew through her mind faster than a run-away stage coach.

Sitting in the sun room with a glass of sherry, she checked off a mental list of all the things she had done to try and get the man's attention. *He is insufferable. How can he ignore me?*

Sylvia considered her options and found each one had failed in attracting the old geezer into her web. *I'm running out of ideas, nothing works.* Holding the sherry with both hands, she stood and paced the room.

She muttered to herself, "I have been a congenial host, complimented him on multiple occasions, allowed bits of skin to show for his benefit, I have even been pleasant with the staff and yet he has ignored me. I had his favorite foods prepared, gathered knowledge about the foundry so we could talk of its future growth." She looked at her glass and drained it in one gulp. "I can think of only one thing, I will dress tonight for a seduction and will have him in bed before he realizes what happened."

She left the room smiling, and focused.

"James," she called, "Prepare me a hot bath, with rose petals."

James' voice roused her from the relaxing soak. Erich had returned from the foundry. Sylvia knew his routine … change clothing, wash up, go down and read the papers, complete any correspondence while drinking a beer.

Always the proper-gentleman, he gave her privacy, after all, as he had said many times, "I have invaded

your home, you deserve your personal peace and quiet."
At times, they would sit and talk, usually about the
foundry, and he never spoke of family. Dinner would be
announced at six. They would eat together. Erich went
to bed soon after dinner.

"But not tonight, dear Erich. Tonight, I will possess
you." she whispered while dressing.

CHAPTER
NINETEEN

The bell chimed at exactly six to announce dinner is served.

Sylvia made her way to the dining room for a grand entrance in her best gown, of form fitting, cherry-red velvet. As she entered, Erich's gaze focused on the plunging neck-line accentuating her large globes. He stood behind her chair to hold it while she sat.

He lingered a couple extra seconds. *I wonder if he is enjoying the view.*

They ate most of the meal without speaking, but

sneaking peaks at one another. She gave him her best 'baby girl' smile, coy yet both innocent while sexually inviting.

Erich remained silent. He would nod when she spoke, but made no move to garner her attention beyond the quick stares.

At the end of the meal, they remained in the dining room for their coffee rather than retiring to the sitting room, as was their usual habit.

Erich turned his chair toward her.

"Mrs. Davlen ... Sylvia ... Your home and the attention you have paid me has made this an enjoyable eight months. But my work here is all but done. I have permanently upgraded the foremen and given the position of plant manager to Mr. Wallace. Everyone has moved up the ranks one spot with a healthy pay raise. Two new men are being sought to take over the night shift position and float between shifts. I am leaving all other plant decisions to Frank. He will send monthly reports to my office and will call me if anything unusual or an accident happens in the building."

Sylvia felt the blood drain from her face. "You're leaving--aren't you?" She whispered.

"Yes, tomorrow on the noon train. I have other business to attend to but will visit once or twice a year as I do all my companies."

Sylvia leaned forward, "Erich Mot, I can't bear the thought of you leaving, but if you must, I understand. Business, of course, always comes first with you, even before your own personal pleasures." She wiped an invisible tear with her napkin.

"I must become unladylike and bold. You are leaving and I have had these … these feeling for you for months." Her hand ran down his arm. "I am a woman with desires and needs. Make me your secret wife. Take my body and soul. I will remain here and long for your visits. I am a lonely widow and have such desire for you."

Her guest studied her for several moments, his gaze raked over her.

"I have no need for a secret wife or mistress. No time with all my travels." He said with a bone chilling smile. "But I must say we would have a most interesting life together."

For the first time since arriving, he removed his gloves and clasped her hands. Sylvia's eyes widened and her lips formed a surprised 'O' as she saw past the illusion of a man of flesh and blood.

Spector grinned as her pupils became fixed and she struggled for her last breaths.

Erich Mot laid her head on the table and stood. Stroking her hair he said, "Yes Sylvia. You are my wife … Mrs. Sylvia Mot … Mrs. Death."

OTHER WORKS
BY
JOHN W. SMITH

These books are also available on Kindle.

Nightmares of a Madman

https://www.amazon.com/dp/0989181006/

Dark Dreams

https://www.amazon.com/dp/0989181049/

Tainted Blood

https://www.amazon.com/dp/0989181057/

Short stories available on Kindle only

Spirit Dagger

https://www.amazon.com/dp/B00JANUU4E/

Colonial Scum

https://www.amazon.com/dp/B00N27GJA8/

Hungry Things

https://www.amazon.com/dp/B00ODJ2ILI

ABOUT THE AUTHOR

JOHN SERVED TWENTY-FIVE YEARS IN THE MILITARY, COMPLETING HIS TOUR AS AN AWARD WINNING JOURNALIST IN THE AIR FORCE RESERVE. AFTER MILITARY RETIREMENT, HE BOUGHT A HARLEY AND BECAME A REGULAR CONTRIBUTOR TO A VARIETY OF LOCAL MOTORCYCLE PUBLICATIONS IN CALIFORNIA AND INTERNATIONAL MAGAZINES. HE LATER RETURNED TO ILLINOIS WHERE HE FINISHED HIS CIVILIAN CAREER IN GERIATRIC CARE. AFTER RETIRING FROM CIVILIAN LIFE, HE ACCEPTED

THE CHALLENGE TO WRITE BOOKS AND STORIES FOR PUBLICATIONS.

BEING A SHORT STORY WRITER, HE PUBLISHED TWO BOOKS OF DARK FICTION HORROR SHORT STORIES AS WELL AS COORDINATING THE PUBLICATION OF AN ANTHOLOGY INVOLVING SEVENTEEN WRITERS. HE HAS ALSO PUBLISHED THREE SHORT STORIES ON KINDLE. TAINTED BLOOD, HIS FIRST NOVEL, WAS PUBLISHED IN 2017. HE IS WORKING ON TWO ADDITIONAL NOVELS AND SEVERAL SHORT STORIES

JOHN W. SMITH

www.ingramcontent.com/pod-product-compliance
Lightning Source LLC
Chambersburg PA
CBHW020626130626
46552CB00003B/1102